THORNS IN MY HEART
ROSES IN MY SOUL

POEMS BY

RACHEL ELLA RICHARDSON

My poetry comes from the heart and
reflects my journey as a woman through
the uncertainty of love; from passion to
heartache, hurt to healing and
powerlessness to empowerment
and finding the strength and courage
to love again.

Rachel Ella Richardson

To all the lovers in the world and to anyone who has ever had their heart broken and thought they could never love again.

Contents

THORNS IN MY HEART
ROSES IN MY SOUL

POEMS

Under

Meet me under
the moonlight sky;
we'll dance in a way
that only the stars understand.

Meet me under
the willow tree;
we'll share a secret
as old as time.

Meet me under
a blanket of flowers;
we'll lose ourselves in
the essence of love.

Ecstasy

You love me
perfectly.

Sun

When

I

leave

your side

it's like

the parting of the sun.

I look forward to

a time

when

I will never have

to watch

another

sunrise or sunset

without

you.

Love Is

Love

isn't

a flower

that

blossoms in the spring.

Love is

a rose

that

continues to bloom

through winter's

harsh and lonely nights.

Love is a beautiful garden

where a thousand

flowers can be found

but only two find

each other.

I vow from this day forward

to

always be your rose

and love you

on

winter's coldest night

and

on

spring's warmest day.

That is how

you will know

that my love

will always bloom

for you.

Robin

Wounded

and

begging

for respite from your own

misery and self-pity.

You spoke of

virtue

but the wings of

truth and respect

had long since taken flight

and

vices of steel coils and

deception and greed

were now your hosts.

I wish to leave you,

in

your current state

as

I never did care much for

wounded birds.

Love Light

You will meet someone

who lives amongst

the sun.

In the meantime

stop associating

with

shadows.

Flourish

I planted you
like a scarlet rosebud in the soil,
like the earth beneath my fingertips.

I can't wait to see you grow
and watch your beauty unfold.

Heartbeat

Tonight I will wear nothing

but magnolias

in my hair

as your cosmic sun-dance

eyes drink in

every inch

of my skin;

the moon is swimming

with every heartbeat

of mine.

Tonight

is made for lovers.

You

Put your head

on my shoulder

and

tell me

who you are.

Forever

As gentle as an evening rose

before the break of dawn,

for summer always seems to take

forever

when the one you love

is gone.

Vows of the Moon to Her Sun

"I promise to always be your moon," she said

as she closed her soft white glow

around

her stars

for the last time that evening.

She waited all night to see the sun,

for to catch a quick

glimpse of the bright orb

would be all she needed to sustain herself

another night.

And as she drifted into the morning's light

she imagined herself to be

a yellow sunflower

basking in the warmth

of the rays of her sun.

Vows of the Sun to His Moon

A deep ray caught the morning sky.
"I promise to always be your sunshine
and your light," said the sun,
for he was thinking of his sweet moon.

"Oh, how I wish you were a sunflower;
you could spend all day
basking in my light,
and I'd pass the time
admiring your beauty."

Instead, he made a vow
that only a sun can make.

"I vow to guide your way

even

in the eve of the night,

for all the stars

that shine

in the evening sky

are there to watch over you,

keep you safe and shining bright,

for you shall

always be

my sweetest moonlight delight."

The sun turned his warm beam

towards a beautiful field of sunflowers and

imagined his

sweet moon

was amongst them.

I Wish

My heart will always miss you.

My eyes will always look for you.

My hand will always long for yours.

I wish I could have loved you longer.

Golden Hour

When you wouldn't

even

give me

the time of day,

how did I end up giving

you

all my

sunrises and sunsets?

The Way We Were

A heartbeat

a handshake

a long embrace

smooth lips

and sliding hips

soothing words

and soft promises

make their way inside my mind.

How to Spot the One

You know a heartache is on the horizon

when the only thing you can think about

is the soothing sound of

his voice

and the gentle touch of

his hand

meeting yours.

You Are Precious and You Are Loved

You are precious and you are loved;
not like some winged bird
loved only for its wings
or for the gift of flight.

You are precious and you are loved;
like a lover
who would do anything
to be by your side
and admire the rise and fall of
your breath,
as it leaves the chambers of your lungs.

You are precious and you are loved;
not like a lion
who's love is born
out of the fear of others
who wants to remain alive for the last time.

You are precious and you are loved;

like a man who realizes that he

is

in fact

in love

for the first time

with a woman

who is happy to watch the fire

in his eyes

dance all night long.

A Promise to the Ocean

Each

wave of

hurt

brings me

closer to the shores

of love.

River

There is now a river between us.
I don't know how we got here.

In between the roses of love
grew brambles and sharp thorns.

No love
can
live here.

Joker

Let me not be fooled

again

by

love.

Seas

A mermaid
and a man;
fingers of flesh
tail of a fin.

He always was
enchanted
by her seas

and she
by his land.

Though
no matter how they might try
scales cannot love skin.

Tonight

Moon beam haze

and

starlight gaze

be my soft warm glow tonight.

Wrap my hair in jasmine

and

lay

scarlet roses at my feet.

Tonight

I am a woman

in

love.

Two Paths

One day you will tell me

all the things I want to hear.

One day you will pronounce

your love for me;

tell me that

I am

the most beautiful woman

you have ever seen.

One day you will decide

that you never want to spend another

hour without my soft skin against your hand.

I am yours forever

in all the seconds of moments

in time.

Stay the course and see

where we lead each other

in love.

This Is Not the End

I promise.
This is not the end.

It might not feel
as if
there is a reason
why,
right
now.

It might feel
that there
is no hope.

But I promise;
you have every
reason to
rise and live
another day,
for in tomorrow,
lies a new
beginning.

How

When the love is gone
how will I learn to love again?

When life is so hard
how do I survive?

When you said,
no
to me
how did I end up saying, yes?

When you are my heart
how will I learn to live without you?

Caught

When you find yourself getting caught

between

the devil and the deep blue sea,

remember that there is

so much

beauty in the world

that goes unseen.

Always search for what you love in life

and

what makes

you

happy.

Moments

Falling in love

with

all the moments

we

share together

keeps me

falling in love

over

and

over again.

Silver Ties

You made me

feel like

a sweet glass of

velvet

wine,

with notes of

cherry.

Lips

budding at the

chance to linger

on my skin;

your winding

words moving

through my

eager heart.

You are an old

vine.

Midnight

My tears
are always
trying to find
their
true selves.

Wave

I feel so much

of who we could

have been;

two wild

horses

running across

the shores.

But the sad truth

is,

we mixed

together

like sugar and

sand.

Fractured Love

I don't want

a fractured love.

I want a love

as deep as the ocean.

I want a love

that is willing to drown me;

gasping

for

air

and

bring me back

to life

all in the same breath.

Your Love in Life

I will

always be

your love in life,

for a thousand times

my heart

dreamed

of yours

before we even met.

I will

always be

your love in life

for

my soul

knew yours

in the same way

the moon

knows the stars.

I will

always be

your love in life

for

I want no one else in

this lifetime

to call mine

but

you.

Trails

The last time

I saw you

was in May,

clutching a field of wildflowers

in my hand

trying my hardest

to hold onto

a love

that I knew was never really

mine.

As the tiger lily sunset fades

deep into the night

violet tears run down my face;

knowing

now

that even

love

runs out of time.

I Miss You

I know

there

is

no more

us,

but I miss

the way

you

used

to make

me

feel.

Move On

Static pictures

run

through

my mind

of the last time

I was with you.

Wild mustangs

race

through

my heart

whenever I

think of you.

I am tired

of you

running and

racing

through my soul.

Fantasy

I will always be in

love

with

the dream

of what

could have been.

But

you

live off alabaster

lies

cloaked

in a life of sin.

Summertime Love

A summer breeze drifts through my window

and I know

you are here with me.

Sensuality

is the key.

Turn me over and over and over again.

Lock me deep in

the chambers

of

your heart.

Am I your secret to keep away

and unlock

whenever

you find

your

pink desires

are too much to bear?

Skin on skin

wind to wind.

I was never yours.

And,

like a soft summer breeze

I am gone again.

Thorns

As I pull my rose-colored bedding
from my mattress
I am reminded of the last time I pulled you
into bed.

As I lay myself down to sleep
I pray this queen has the strength to never let
that joker into her chambers again.

I will slumber deep
and dream of my king.

Roses are beautiful,
but their thorns can be deadly.

My King

You feel like sunshine

on a warm day in May.

Your touch could heal

the darkest demons

of my soul.

Your love flows

through me

like the sweet perfume of jasmine

on a summer's night.

I know you are out there

in the universe

my king.

Your queen is waiting for you.

Then There Was Love

I don't want electricity,
for love
is all the power
I need.

Golden Days

Reach for your dreams.

They are on the other side

where the butterflies live.

Amber wings spread out;

soft lilies cradle me

as I soar through

the wild ceaon

Let each dewdrop flower

be my friend

and a spindled cloud

be my guide.

I want to be a butterfly.

I Met You in Summertime

Bold sunflowers

basking

in their golden days;

green earth mounts

and

cool blue skies

rule the day.

In this moment

cherry lips and soft amber hair

unite my heart with yours.

Summertime love is easy to find.

Your words seduce me and tell me everything

I will ever need to know.

A warm hand moves to mine

and lovers know the rest.

Tell me why

summertime love

is better left undressed.

I Forgive You

To take someone

who you

thought

was

a

lover

but

was really

a

sinner.

I forgive you.

Absence of Nothing

He longed for a clarity and a vision
that would never come
for when we cast our minds in darkness
we forget how to be of the light.

His senses were dulled by a veil
of black and gray
which clouded him.

He could not see the one standing before him
who would restore his sight.

Bloom

You are not a just flower,

for a flower only blooms once.

The scarlet buds will eventually wilt

and

their time will expire.

You are a beautiful garden

full of flowers

and

the sweet nectar of life.

You will bloom

many times

in this

lifetime

and

only you can choose

where you want to be planted.

Home

Marry someone

who has

the heart

of a

tree.

Lush emerald

leaves;

their rustling

promise

to always

listen to you.

Branches wrap

around you;

an oath

to always stand

by your side.

A knight of
timber.
A prince of the
woods.
A king among all
forests.

Marry someone
who has
the heart
of a
tree.

Vibe

Current mood:
peaceful

Guilty

Do you see me as I see you?

As a god.

As an emperor.

As a savior.

Am I your goddess?

Your queen?

Your saint?

How can you be

my

savior

when all we do

is sin?

Letting Go

When the last evening lark
sings its song for the night
and the first star
glimmers in the sky,
I know you are no longer mine.

Love Me True and Love Me Long

I long to feel your warm touch
move across my hand.
Your full lips are blushing
and I am not a shy woman.

When it's just you and I
and we are tangled up together
getting lost in heavy breaths and
promises
that I know
neither
of us is going to keep,
I feel like
a
scarred lover.

Remember Who You Are

Beautiful woman

let me

tell you who you are

in case

your mother never told you,

when you were a little girl

at night

before she

tucked you into bed.

Being a woman

is

a

gift

more sacred than

any

diamond or gold trinket.

I will tell you

a secret

more ancient

than the oldest grain of sand.

Know your

regal power.

You

are

a Queen.

Feel your

inner love.

You

are

a Goddess.

Sense your

divine strength.

You are

a Warrior.

This is who

you

have

always been.

This is what you will demand

and why

you will not settle

for

anything

less.

It is

your birthright;

Woman.

New Dawn

In the cool dawn of the morning

she remembered

who

she

was

and left behind

all that she

had

been.

Rise now.

It is

your

time.

Goddess Status

You know you are a true goddess
when
you can bask in the bliss of the gorgeous nectar of
a peach
allowing it's plump sweet fruit to nourish your
body.

You know you are a goddess
when
your favorite song comes on
and you allow its musical waves
to fill your ears and mind with sensual delight.

You know you are a goddess
when
you find the perfect dress to wear
and you can walk proudly
holding your head high
knowing you are embracing your divine femininity.

You know you are a goodness

when

you can say

no

to anyone who doesn't treat you

with love

respect

and honor.

Find your inner goodness

and

make her your priority

every

day!

Good Morning Beautiful One

Today

will you choose to be a

tidal wave?

Salty fingertips grabbing a life you know you are

owed.

A furious crash transcending

every room you enter

letting every

urchin and barnacle

know

that

you

are here to stay.

Mermaid tendril hair

communes with starfish

telling them your

hopes and dreams

while an unwavering convoy

of

fanciful delight

glides across the calm ocean waters

waiting a reply from the sea.

I hear

a

"Yes you may."

Today

I will be

a

tidal wave.

Speak This Now

To all my girls

who would be princesses,

to all my ladies

who grew

up to be queens,

speak this now

and feel it from the depths of your soul.

You deserve better,

the best.

They say the best is yet to come.

Well here you are

watching, waiting and yearning

for a better life than the one you have now.

Will a cool wind set forth your dreams

on a luminous cloud set deep in the sun?

Will the moon beam haze drift your desires into a
restful chamber
of blissful slumber?
Will you then awaken to have your fantasies laid
before you on a silver platter?

You must
be it
will it
create it.

Like a flower bursts from a tiny seed
in the earth
so you must unearth your deepest fantasies.
Call it
into creation
into essence
into light
into form.

From this moment on
this is how
you will run your life.

Speak it.
Will it.
Be it.

My golden one,
your deepest request
is being answered.
All you have to do
is will it forward
and
call it in.
It just is.

Your Time

A gold crown

is placed on her head.

Rubies and diamonds adorn its golden house.

Long radiant hair surrounds it

like angels in a cathedral.

Rise now.

It

is your

time to

lead,

Queen.

Sweet Child Inside

Sweet one

I choose to heal

to release

any negative energy

from my soul.

I take back

my power.

I know my own right.

I decide

who

I allow into my life

and

what kind of life

I want to have.

You are in charge

of your destiny sweet one.

The time is NOW.

Make a Wish

You can't lie to the moon.

She knows

every

saint's

secret lust

and

every sinner's

darkest desire;

a serene kiss

from a

silver-tongued lover

with stardust

in your eyes.

Make a wish.

Lead

Recalling what it's like;

so heart-broken beyond words.

Understanding that the past

is what followed me

to the future.

Acceptance for the present;

it's so hard to be alone.

Absence is the prize of loss.

Resentment is a close second.

Recalling what it's like

to open hearts and know

that tomorrow

may be not mean today

that yesterday is gone

and all we have is time

and what we want when morning comes
and who we need as the sun shines
through our window.

Be my way.

Divine Love

Love me with a
soft touch;
the way a
pianist's
fingertips
lovingly
graze
its black and
ivory keys.

The way an
angelic prophet
speaks words
of truth and
wisdom that
make you feel
safe when
you have been
afraid
for so long.

Love me the way

a gardener

carefully clips his roses

and delicately

places them into

a vase,

with

fresh water

and

sunlight to

thrive.

The way a

painter strokes

his

brush

across

the canvas

and watches the

colors fly.

Love me the way

a singer

sings those

sweet

notes

that make you

feel young again

and like you just

cannot stop

dancing.

Now THAT

is a love

worth

waiting for!

Waiting

I want
a
viscous love.

Almost Everything

On a stranded edge
waking only to find that I was in a haze
still dreaming of a day
I could be something to some
and everything to one.

You're still living life
like a bladed weapon
holding in on your chance to beam bright.

If I'm something
think of me
as a star
that glimmers in the deep dark sky.
For a short time I'll light your way
but I'll burn out one day.

If I'm everything,

then I'm a warm filtered light

that grazes your skin

and flutters through your eyes.

That's just light's way of letting you know

that I will always shine.

A Rose's Word of Wisdom

Pink and lavender

Sweet pea blossoms rise up

and perfume the sky

with their floral aroma.

A single fuzzy honey bee

circles the garden.

He rounds at each rose

in search of

the flower

with the most potent nectar.

Let this be a healing to all men:

Your woman

is not just another pretty flower

growing in a garden

grown only for you to

pluck and replace

with a new bright bloom

once her petals start to fade.

Get to know her essence

and you will come to

understand

what makes her

soul sway in the wind

and

her heart bloom

like

the

wild rose she is.

A Rosebud's Vow

A rosebud made a vow

to never

open her petals

to the warmth

of the sun

for fear

she might learn to

live, love and perish

all in a season's time.

Love

Wild vines live in

your veins.

Jade green

stems

and

soft feathered

leaves

wind

their way to your

heart

where a single

flaming rose

blooms.

This

is why

I love you.

Walk Two Moons

If we all run out of hope
one day,

pretend love doesn't exist,

turn my face away,

Refuse your kiss.

If we all run on empty
movin' forward on a prayer,
hold onto the past,
act like my heart just ain't there.

Walk two moons.

Climb down that dusty road
take my shoes,
make them your own.

Walk two moons.

Shed your skin,
tell those lights it's okay
to go down dim;
you know the way home anyway.

Walk two moons
one day.

Onward

I am willing to look past it
and love
all over again.

About Me

I live in Santa Cruz, California with my English Spot rabbit, Domino, and enjoy writing poetry, drawing, painting, yoga, walking on the beach, hiking and picking flowers.   I studied Art at the California College of the Arts in Oakland, California and received a BS in Psychology from California State University, Monterey Bay.   I work in the field of mental health with elder adults, as a social worker.

Follow me on:

and email me at

Rachel@RachelEllaRichardson.com

Made in the USA
Middletown, DE
13 September 2021